ISBN 0 86112 823 0
© Brimax Books Ltd 1992. All rights reserved.
Published by Brimax Books Ltd, Newmarket, England 1992.
Printed in Italy.

Wind in the Willows

Illustrated by Eric Kincaid

BRIMAX BOOKS · NEWMARKET · ENGLAND

Introduction

Kenneth Grahame's *The Wind in the Willows* is one of the best loved classics of children's literature. It tells the enchanting story of the Mole, the Water Rat, Badger and the roguish but lovable Toad.

One sunny spring morning the Mole finds himself by the river bank for the first time. There he meets Ratty, with whom he becomes very good friends, and together they explore the beauty of the river bank. Ratty introduces the Mole to Badger who lives deep in the Wild Wood, and to Toad of Toad Hall. Together they share many adventures.

But disaster strikes when the Toad, because of his passion for motor cars, finds himself in prison. Before he can plan his escape Toad Hall is invaded by the Wild Wooders, an evil gang of ferrets, stoats and weasels.

Although the Mole, Ratty and Badger try to defend Toad's home, it is not until Toad himself returns, that the final battle can be fought.

This specially adapted version of *The Wind in the Willows* has been lovingly illustrated by Eric Kincaid. Younger readers will be enchanted as they follow the adventures of the four animal friends.

Contents

Chapter	Page
The River Bank	8
The Open Road	13
The Wild Wood and Mr Badger	18
Home Sweet Home	25
The Adventures of Mr Toad	30
'Like Summer Tempests Came His Tears'	46
The Return of the Hero	55

The River Bank

The Mole had been busy all morning. He was spring-cleaning his little home.

Spring was in the air and the Mole had suddenly had enough.

"Bother!" he said. He threw down his paint brush and ran straight out of his little house into the glorious sunshine outside.

"Oh, this is much better," he cried, as he ran along the grassy paths and across the green meadows. The sound of bird-song filled the air as he skipped along. All around him was busy with the arrival of spring.

He wandered aimlessly along when he came to a river. He had never seen a river before. The river gurgled and chuckled, chased and ran past the spot on the bank where he stood. The Mole was enchanted! He walked along the bank as the river ran by, then he sat and watched.

As he looked across the river, he suddenly noticed a dark opening on the opposite bank. Deep in the opening he saw a face with twinkling eyes. The face came further out of the hole. Such a glossy coat, such neat ears. It was the Water Rat!

"Hullo, Mole!" said the Water Rat.

"Hullo, Rat!" said the Mole.

"Would you like to come over?" asked the Rat, after a pause.

"Easier said than done, I think," said the Mole. who knew next to nothing about riverside life.

The Rat said nothing, but bent down and untied a rope; he then stepped into a small boat that the Mole had not noticed. The Rat rowed across the river.

"Jump in," said the Rat. "Quickly, now." He held out his paw for the Mole to take. The Mole stepped gingerly into the boat and sat down.

The Rat began to row to the opposite bank.

"This is my first time in a boat," said the Mole.

"What!" cried the Rat. "What have you been doing, then?"

"Is it that good?" asked the Mole, from the comfort of the cushions at the back of the boat, already convinced that it was.

"It's the best," said the Rat, dreamily. "Just floating, doing nothing. It's the only thing to do."

"Rat! Look out!" the Mole cried, as the small boat ran into the bank. The dreamer ended up flat on his back, heels in the air, smiling to himself.

"Just messing," he sighed. "Look here! If you've nothing better to do, how do you fancy making a day of just drifting down the river."

"What a day I'm having," the Mole sighed. "Can we go now?"

The Rat smiled and moored up the boat. He climbed up into his hole, returning with a well-packed picnic basket.

"Shove that under your feet," he said to the Mole, as he passed it down into the boat.

"What's inside?" asked the Mole, as he looked at the basket.

"Oh, a bit of everything," said the Rat. "Cold chicken, coldtonguecoldhamcoldbeefpickledgherkhins saladfrenchrollscresssandwichespottedmeatginger beerlemonadesodawater –"

9

*"Shove that under your feet," he said to the Mole,
as he passed it down into the boat.*

"This is all too much!" the Mole cried.

"Do you really think so?" asked the Rat.

The Mole was trailing a paw in the water.

"What's over there?" asked the Mole after a while, as the Rat rowed them past a wood on one side of the river.

"That," said the Rat, "is the Wild Wood. We river bankers hardly ever go there. The Badger lives right in the heart of the wood and no one would bother him."

"Bother him?" asked the Mole.

"Well, there are foxes, weasels and stoats," said the Rat. "I've aways got on all right with them, but they do sometimes break out."

"What's beyond that?" asked the Mole.

"The wide world," said the Rat. "I've never been there and I don't plan to go. Neither should you. Now, here's somewhere for our picnic."

The Rat turned into the bank and moored. In no time, the Mole, amid 'oohs' and 'aahs' of pleasure, unwrapped the mysterious tasty parcels within the hamper.

The two new friends set to on the feast.

"What are you looking at?" asked the Rat, after a while, when the Mole could finally pull himself away from the picnic cloth.

"It's a stream of bubbles," said the Mole.

At that moment, a broad muzzle broke the surface of the water and the Otter appeared. He came up out of the river and headed straight for the picnic cloth.

"You greedy beggars," he said when he saw the remains of the food. "Why didn't you invite me?"

"Totally unplanned," said the Rat. "By the way, this is my friend, Mr Mole."

"Delighted, I'm sure," said the Otter. There was a sudden rustle behind them and a stripey head appeared from the bushes.

"Badger!" cried the Rat. "Do join us."

"Company," muttered the Badger and he rustled away.

"Oh, well," said the Rat, a little disappointed. "Tell us, Otter, who else is on the river?"

11

"Toad for one," said the Otter. "In his brand new canoe."

The Otter and the Rat laughed together. At that moment a splashing could be heard from the river. All three looked to see a stout fellow row past.

The Otter's attention was suddenly diverted by a rather large mayfly. A quick splash into the river and he was gone.

"Time for us to go, too," said the Rat. The two got into the boat and the Rat gently rowed them back down the river. The Mole sat looking at the Rat and the easy way with which the boat moved.

"Let me have a go, Ratty," the Mole said.

"Not yet," said the Rat. "It's not as easy as it looks."

The Mole sat for a minute or two, watching and then suddenly made a grab for the oars. The Rat was taken completely by surprise and ended up in the bottom of the boat.

The Mole started to row, not really knowing how to.

"You'll have us over!" cried the Rat. The Mole missed the water with the oars and threw himself off balance. The boat went with him and Sploosh! Everything went flying and the Mole ended up in the river.

He was going down for a second time when he felt the Rat grab him and drag him to shore.

"I'm very sorry, Ratty," said the Mole.

"Don't worry," said the Rat. "What's water to a Water Rat? I'm just as at home in it as out of it. Besides, it looks like we will have to teach you to swim and to row a boat, but all in good time. Home now."

The Rat took the Mole home and setting the fire, made him very comfortable until supper, told him tales of river life and the animals that live by the river.

After supper, a very tired Mole was escorted to the best bedroom and there he slept, knowing that the river lapped at the windowsill. It was a start of a very busy summer for the Mole and the Rat.

12

The Open Road

"Ratty," said the Mole, one beautiful summer morning. "Can I ask you for a favour?"

Ratty was not paying much attention to the Mole. He had spent the morning playing in the river with the ducks and had annoyed them so much they asked him to leave them alone. He now sat composing a song for his friends. It went something like this:

All along the backwater,
Through the rushes tall,
Ducks are a-dabbling,
Up tails all!

Ducks' tails, drakes' tails,
Yellow feet a-quiver,
Yellow bills all out of sight
Busy in the river!

Slushy green undergrowth
Where the roach swim –
Here we keep our larder,
Cool and full and dim.

Every one for what he likes!
We like to be
Heads down, tails up,
Dabbling free!

High in the blue above
Swifts whirl and call –
We are down a-dabbling
Up tails all!

"I don't think too much of that," said the Mole.

"Neither did the ducks," said the Rat.

"Look Ratty," said the Mole. "I've heard so much about Mr Toad. When will you take me to see him?"

"No better time than now," said Ratty. "Come on. We'll get the boat and paddle up."

Turning a bend in the river, the Mole had his first sight of Toad Hall.

"It's one of the nicest on the river," said the Rat, "but we don't tell Toad that."

They moored the boat in the boat-house. It was empty.

"Oh, well," said the Rat. "Looks like boating is out of favour at the moment."

The two friends strolled across the gardens, they soon found Toad poring over a large map.

"Splendid!" cried Toad. "I was just about to send for you, Ratty. Come inside."

"Hang on, Toady," said the Rat. "Let's just sit a moment."

He sat in one of the easy chairs. The Mole sat in the other, saying to Toad how lovely he thought Toad Hall was.

"Finest on the river," said Toad, who immediately turned red as he saw the Rat nudge the Mole's foot. "All right, Ratty, you know me. Anyway, I'm glad you're both here."

"Need help with the rowing, is that it?" asked the Rat.

"Oh, pooh! Boating!" exclaimed Toad. "I gave that up long ago. No, this is the real thing, the only way to spend your days. Come with me and I will show you both what I mean."

Toad led the pair to the stableyard. There, standing in front of the coach-house, was a beautiful canary yellow gipsy caravan. It was picked out in red and green.

"There!" cried Toad. "This is real life. Out on the road in this, here today and off tomorrow and an ever-changing horizon! Have a look!"

The Mole was very interested and followed Toad up the steps and peeked inside. The Rat stayed where he was.

"Everything is in here," said Toad. "Everything ready for when we start this afternoon."

"I beg your pardon," said the Rat. "Did I hear words like 'we' and 'start' and 'this afternoon'?"

"Now, Ratty," said Toad, imploringly. "You've got to come. I can't possibly manage without you."

"I don't care," said the Rat. "I'm not coming."

The Mole was disappointed as he had fallen in love with the little caravan. His glum face spoke volumes to the Rat, who was really kind-hearted and very fond of the Mole.

"Come in and have something to eat," said Toad. "We'll talk it over."

Lunch was excellent and Toad let himself go. He painted wonderful pictures of the open road to the Mole. Finally the Rat was brought round. He didn't really want to hurt his two friends.

After lunch, the triumphant Toad led the way back to the coach-house and the caravan. Between them, they caught the reluctant horse who was to pull the caravan around the countryside.

It was a golden afternoon and friends waved as they went by.

Evening came and they stopped to make their camp.

"Give me this rather than your old river, any day," said Toad, as they lay in their bunks that night.

"It's not my old river," sighed the Rat. "But I do miss it."

"If you like, we can go home tomorrow," whispered the Mole.

"No, better not," said the Rat. "No saying what will happen if Toady is left on his own."

The following day, the Mole was driving the caravan and the Rat and Toad walked behind. A distant hum behind them developed into a distinct buzz, but all they could see was a cloud of dust. Then a faint 'Poop-poop!' could be heard.

The Rat and Toad turned to continue their conversation, when suddenly, they all leapt into the nearest ditch, as the motor-car rushed past.

They were left in a cloud of dust, as the motor-car disappeared into the distance.

The old horse was thrown into a total panic and shot the caravan backwards into a ditch. It now lay on its side, a complete wreck. The Mole tried to pacify the horse, the Rat danced up and down, simply transported with passion.

"You villains!" he cried. "You scoundrels! You

The Rat danced up and down
simply transported with passion.

roadhogs! I'll have you! I'll take you to court!"

Meanwhile, Toad sat in the middle of the road, where he had landed. There was a glazed expression on his face and he softly murmered, "Poop-poop! Poop-poop!"

The Rat and the Mole turned to the wreckage.

"Come on, Toad! Give us a hand!" they called.

"What a sight!" murmured Toad. "The real way to travel. Oh bliss. Oh poop-poop! And to think, I didn't know about them. All those wasted years!"

"Come on, Toad!" cried the Rat. "We've got to go to the nearest town and you must report those villains. Then you must find a blacksmith to put the caravan back on the road."

"Report them!" said the dumbstruck Toad. "Me! Complain about that heavenly machine! Mend the caravan! I'm done with caravans. I know what I want now and I owe it all to you two, my friends, I wouldn't have come on this trip myself, without you and then I would have missed it. Those sounds, that smell, that poop-poop!"

"Oh, come on, Mole," said the Rat. "We'll get no more sense out of him today. He's hopeless. We'll both go into town and find the time of the next train to take us home."

On arrival in town, the still-dreaming Toad was left in the waiting room at the station while the Mole and the Rat ensured that the horse was well stabled. The caravan was taken care of and then the three animals took the train home.

The two friends even had to escort Toad home.

The little home in the riverbank was very comfortable and inviting as the two friends settled down to their late supper.

The next day, the Mole had a very lazy time of it and did not get up till late. The Rat had already left and was chatting with his friends along the riverbank.

Later in the day, he found the Mole, fishing.

"Heard the news," he said.

"No, what's that?" asked the Mole.

"Toad went into town first thing this morning and ordered his very own motor-car," said the Rat.

The Wild Wood and Mr Badger

For a long time now, the Mole had wanted to meet the Badger.

"Couldn't you ask him to dinner?" asked the Mole.

But the Rat always seemed to put him off, saying, "He doesn't like company, so he wouldn't come."

"Why don't we visit him, then?" asked the Mole.

"Oh, no," said the Rat. "We can't do that."

Summer had faded and the Autumn days were becoming shorter and cooler, until finally Winter was almost upon them. The Rat slept a great deal in Winter. The Mole had plenty of time on his hands and so, one afternoon while the Rat dozed in front of the fire, the Mole decided to go to the Wild Wood and try to find Mr Badger.

He wrapped up warmly and quietly left the house. He walked between the trees, going further into the wood and it gradually became darker as the trees grew closer together.

A quick glimpse of an evil wedge-shaped little face and the Mole told himself to stop imagining things. But then he saw another, then another – peeping at him from little holes!

The Mole was terrified and he headed deeper into the wood. Then he heard whistling. It came from in front, behind, to the sides – they were all around him!

Then he heard the pattering of small feet and he seemed to be surrounded. He thought of the Rat, sitting in front of his warm fire. A rabbit ran up to him and muttered, "Get out, you fool, get out!"

The Mole listened to the pattering and ran in a panic through the trees and undergrowth, until he could go no further. Finally, he hid himself in the hollow of an old beech tree. He lay there panting and trembling, knowing that the Rat had tried to save him from this.

Meanwhile, back in the cosy hole in the river bank, the Rat had woken up. He turned to ask the Mole something.

"Mole!" he called several times, before he realised that the Mole was not there. He saw that his hat and coat were missing and also the new galoshes, bought for the Winter weather, were gone.

He went outside and could see the tracks made by the galoshes. They headed straight for the Wild Wood. The Rat looked serious for a moment then he went back into his house. He emerged with a couple of pistols and a stout stick. He set off after the footprints.

It was dusk as he reached the wood and he started his search for his friend. The little faces quickly disappeared when they saw the stick that the Rat carried.

"Mole, where are you?" the Rat called, he walked back and forth, for an hour or more looking for the Mole. "Mole, I'm here!"

"Is that you, Ratty?" cried a scared Mole. The Rat followed the Mole's voice and found him in his beech hollow.

"Come on, we'll get you home," said the Rat. "Before it's too dark to see."

"Can I rest for just a moment?" asked the Mole. "I'm exhausted."

"All right," said the Rat. "We'll wait until the moon comes up. You are silly to come here in the first place, Mole. We river bankers don't come here at this time of year."

"I'm sorry, Ratty," said the Mole and he curled up and fell asleep. After a short rest the Mole woke up and felt more his usual self.

"Right, we'll be off then," said the Rat and he put his head out of the entrance to their shelter.

"Well, well," he said quietly to himself.

"What's up?" asked the Mole.

"Snow's up," said the Rat. "Or down, should I say. It's snowing hard."

Both animals looked out of their shelter at the snow-covered wood. It looked so different – not at all the threatening place that the Mole had tried to hide from.

"We can't stay here," said the Rat. "The only thing is, snow makes it all look so different."

It did indeed, but the two friends set out bravely, looking for familiar paths and trees to lead them out of the wood. After an hour or so, they had to stop and rest.

"We can't stay here long," said the Rat. "The snow will soon be too deep for us to walk through. Come on, we'll try that dip and see if there is a cave or somewhere dry for us to rest. It might stop snowing soon."

They were heading for the dip when the Mole suddenly tripped and cut his leg.

"Oh, dear," said the Rat. "You're not having much luck today, are you?"

"It must have been a rock," said the Mole.

"It's a very clean cut," said the Rat. "More as if it were something metal. How strange." He turned from the Mole's leg and began scraping and scratching in the snow.

"Come on," said the Mole. "What are you doing?"

"Just looking," said the Rat. "Just looking for . . . Hooray! I've got it!"

"Got what?" asked the Mole.

"Look!" cried the Rat and he pointed.

"It's a doorscraper," said the puzzled Mole. "So?"

"But don't you see?" said the Rat.

"All I can see is that someone has been very careless," said the Mole.

"Oh, Moly!" cried the Rat. And he continued digging away at the snow. After a few minutes' work, a doormat could be seen.

"Can you really not see?" cried the Rat. "Keep digging if you want to sleep somewhere warm tonight."

The Mole continued to dig, but more to humour the Rat. After a few minutes, the Rat's stick made a hollow sound when prodded into a bank of snow.

There stood a solid green door, with a bell-pull and a brass name plate. Neatly engraved on the name plate were the words: MR BADGER.

The Mole was amazed. "You are so clever!" he cried to the Rat. "If only I could think so . . ."

"But you can't," said the Rat, a bit unkindly.

"Come on, let's pull on the bell-pull and knock and see if anyone is in."

They waited for a few minutes and at last heard the sound of steps shuffling down a long corridor.

"Who is it?" called the Badger. "Fancy disturbing people at this hour. Speak up!"

"Badger, it's me, Rat!" cried the Rat. "Let us in please. I'm with my friend Mole and we lost our way in the snow."

"Why Ratty," exclaimed the Badger. "Come in, you must both be frozen. This isn't the weather for two small animals to be out in," he said. "Up to your usual tricks, eh Ratty?"

He made them sit in front of the fire, with warm, dry dressing gowns on, instead of wet clothes.

Conversation was out of the question while food demanded all their attention. But when they did start to tell him what had happened, the Badger didn't say, "I told you so," or "It would have been better if," or anything like that. The Mole was beginning to like him a lot.

After a while the Badger said, "And how's old Toad?"

"Oh, he's going from bad to worse," said the Rat. "But nobody can tell him. He's on his seventh car now and all the bits of the previous six are in the coach-house."

"He's been in hospital three times," added the Mole. "And the fines he's had to pay!"

"The trouble is," said the Rat. "Toad is rich but he's not a millionaire and he's going to get into serious trouble soon. We ought to do something, Badger. We are his friends."

"Yes, you're right," said the Badger. "But it's the wrong time of year. Later on when the days are longer, we'll sort him out. Now then, Rat, you're asleep."

"Not me!" said the Rat, waking with a jump.

"Time for bed for us all, I think," said the kindly Badger and led the way to his spare room where the two friends crawled between the lavender-scented sheets and drifted off to sleep.

The next morning, the two went to the kitchen for

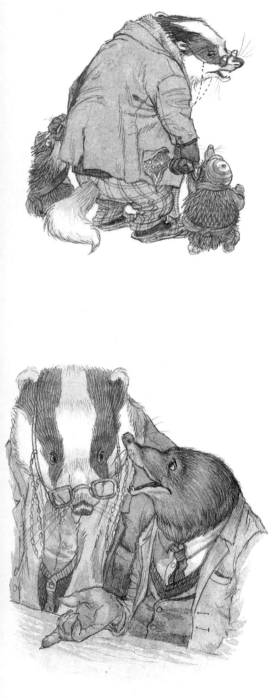

their breakfast. There they found two young hedgehogs who had been lost in the snow and taken in by the Badger.

"How's the weather?" asked the Rat.

"Bad, sir, terribly deep the snow is," they told him.

"Where's Mr Badger?" asked the Mole.

"He's retired to his study, sir," replied the hedgehog. "Not to be disturbed, he said."

"Aah," said the Rat. Everyone realised that this meant that following a hearty breakfast, the Badger now had his feet up in front of a fire and was fast asleep.

The door-bell clanged and the younger hedgehog was sent to investigate. It was the Otter and he threw his arms around the Rat.

"Thought I'd find you here," he said. "Everyone on the river bank is in a right panic – no Rat and no Mole and all this snow. So where do people go when they need help – Mr Badger, so here I am! The Wild Wood does look beautiful though. Snow-castles and snow-caverns have sprung up from nowhere in the night. I even found the rabbit who warned Mole to get out of the wood."

"Weren't you frightened at all?" asked the Mole.

"Frightened?" laughed the Otter, "I'd show them what it's like to be frightened. Do fry me some of that bacon, Mole, there's a good chap."

The Mole set the hedgehogs to frying more bacon while the two friends chatted. Badger entered, yawning and stretching as a second plate of bacon was being prepared.

"Ah good, Otter," said Badger. "You'll stay for lunch of course. And now I must take these two hedgehogs home."

Over lunch, the Rat and the Otter were still deep in river-gossip, so the Mole was delighted to have the opportunity to talk to Mr Badger.

Both agreed that underground was by far the best place to live. The Badger beamed at the Mole.

"Imagine being Rat. A couple of feet of flood water and he's got to move into rented lodgings! What about Toad in that Hall. Beautiful house, I agree,

*"Snow-castles and snow-caverns have sprung up
from nowhere in the night."*

but what if there's a fire? What happens to Toad? We're at home underground. It's much better down here. Tell you what, after lunch, I'll take you round and show you the place."

The Mole was delighted and in due course, the two set off through the Badger's corridors. The Mole was astonished to see the size of the place and the solid stone ceilings, pillars and pavements.

"How did you do it all?" the amazed Mole asked.

"Well to be honest, I didn't," said the Badger. "Oh, I cleaned up bits, storerooms and the like, but it was all here. Years ago, where the Wild Wood is now, there was a city, it is still here but all the people are long gone. The trees grew and now I live here. By the way, I shall pass the word to those who need to know that you are welcome in the wood. Any friend of mine walks where he wants to or I know the reason why."

They headed back to the kitchen and found the Rat dressed and ready to leave. He was looking forward to seeing his home and the river again. Being underground for so long was making him nervous.

"Come along, Mole," he said when he saw the two return. "We must leave while it's still daylight."

"It's all right, Ratty," said the Otter. "I'll be with you, there won't be any bother."

"You've no need to worry, Ratty," added the Badger. "My tunnels go further than you think. I have a few, little known escape routes to outside the Wild Wood, so you needn't even walk through the trees again. When you're ready, we'll leave."

The Rat was ready and quite keen to get back to his river there and then, so the Mole dressed himself warmly again and the Badger led the way down one of his corridors that seemed to go on for miles. They emerged at the edge of the wood and after a hasty goodbye, the Badger covered the exit and disappeared.

The Otter led the way across the fields towards the river, leaving behind the dark shadows of the Wild Wood. They were soon at home, by a warm fire, with the familiar sounds of the river running by the window.

Home Sweet Home

The two friends had been out for the day and now were making their way home across the fields. They found a path that lead to a real road.

"There'll be a village ahead," said the Mole.

"Never mind," said the Rat. "Everyone will be inside in this weather."

They had a quick look in some of the windows as they passed and everything looked cosy and warm. A sudden gust of sleet made them realise how far they had to get to their own warm and cosy sitting room.

They plodded on, out of the village and headed once more across the fields. The Mole was thinking a good deal about supper and was trailing behind the Rat who marched on in the direction of home. The Rat therefore did not notice the poor Mole when the call reached him. It was like an electric shock. He stopped dead in his tracks, his nose quivering and snuffling the air. Home! That was what was calling him! His cosy little home that he left so suddenly that Spring morning. The home he had forgotten, but which had not forgotten him. It wanted him back.

"Ratty!" called the Mole. "Wait! Hold on!"

"Come on, Mole!" said the Rat, from further down the track.

"Oh, stop please, Ratty," said the Mole. "You don't understand. It's my home. It's calling me. I must go to it. Oh, please Ratty. Come back."

The Rat was by now far ahead of the Mole and couldn't hear what the Mole was saying. "We mustn't stop now, Mole," he called back. "I can smell snow."

The Mole was torn. He didn't like to abandon the Rat, but his home was calling him. He gave a great sob, then turned his back and headed after the Rat. The Rat chatted away about the day and didn't notice his friend's silence. After a while he said, "We'll stop for a short rest. We're nearly home."

The Mole sat on a tree stump and tried to control himself, but he couldn't stop the sob from emerging. Another swiftly followed it, then another and the Rat looked on as the Mole burst into floods of tears.

"What is it, old friend?" he asked. "What can I do?"

The poor Mole found it hard to talk. "Home," he choked. "I know it's small and dark. Not like your cosy home, or Badger's or Toad's Hall, but it's home. It called me. I could smell it, I had to leave it. I thought my heart would break, we could have just taken a look, but you wouldn't come back. I called, but you wouldn't . . ." The Mole burst into tears again.

"We're going to find that home of yours, old fellow," replied the Rat pleasantly. "Now use that nose of yours and find the way."

The Mole and the Rat headed back down the track, the Mole with his nose in the air, sniffing at the wind. Suddenly, the Rat felt the Mole stiffen slightly and waited while the Mole caught the scent again, then the Mole was off, over a field, through the undergrowth and hedges and then he dived into a tunnel. The Rat followed him down.

It seemed a long time to the Rat before the tunnel ended and he could stand again. When they did, the Mole struck a match and lit a lantern. They were standing just outside 'Mole End', the Mole's home.

The Rat looked at the forecourt and saw the garden roller and skittle-alley, the bench and the pond. The Mole was beaming to see his familiar belongings again.

Once inside though, the Mole sat down. The place showed months of disuse.

"Oh, why did I do it, Ratty?" he sighed. "We could be in a warm cosy place by now. Instead we're here."

"But it is cosy," said the Rat, running here and there, looking in cupboards and drawers. "And it will soon be warm. I'll light a fire, you try and smarten things up and dust things off. Come on, it won't take long."

"We're going to find that home of yours, old fellow,"
replied the Rat pleasantly.

Encouraged by his friend, the Mole set to and soon a cheerful fire blazed in the hearth. But then he sat down again. "But what do we eat? Your lovely supper is at home and I've nothing to give you."

A sudden scuffling outside the front door drew their attention. Little voices whispered away.

"What's that?" asked the Rat.

"I think it must be the field-mice," said the Mole. "They're carol-singing and they always come to Mole End last and I give them hot drinks and supper."

"Let's have a look then," said the Rat, jumping up and running to the door.

Outside, standing in the lantern light was a group of eight to ten little field-mice. They shuffled from one foot to the other and as the door opened they burst into song.

When they finished bells could be heard ringing away in the cold night air.

"Well sung, boys," said the Rat. "Now, come into the warm and have something hot."

"Yes, come along, field-mice," cried the Mole eagerly. "This is just like old times! Shut the door after you." Then aside to the Rat he said, "But Ratty, we have nothing to give them."

The Rat had thought of this and had a quick word with the eldest field-mouse and sent him off with a basket and some money. The local shop was open at all hours at this time of year, the field-mouse had said.

The Rat had meanwhile found some bottles of ale and was busy heating them, while the Mole chatted with the field-mice. A short while later, the field-mouse returned with a basket full of goodies. Under the Rat's command everyone was sent to fetch or do something and in no time, supper was ready.

The Mole took a long look at his little home. He knew it wasn't grand and that he didn't want to live here all the time, away from the sunshine and his friends, but he knew that this little place, which was all his, would always be there and that he could always come back to it.

*"Yes, come along, field mice," cried the Mole eagerly.
"This is quite like old times! Shut the door after you."*

The Adventures of Mr Toad

The Mole and the Rat were having breakfast when there was a knock at the door. It was Badger. He strode into the room looking very serious.

"The hour has come," said the Badger.

"What hour?" asked the Rat, looking at the clock.

"Toad's hour," said the Badger. "I said we would wait until Winter was over. Now is the time."

The three friends set off for Toad Hall. When they arrived, there standing in the drive was a gleaming, new, red motor-car.

"Hullo," said Toad. "You're just in time to come for a . . ."

"Take him inside," said Mr Badger. Toad was hustled into the house by the Mole and the Rat.

"You can take the car back," said Mr Badger to the driver. "Mr Toad won't be needing it anymore."

"Now then, Toad," said Mr Badger, in the hall. "You've just gone too far. We'll have a chat in the study and see if you come out the same Toad that goes in."

He led Toad in to the study and shut the door.

"I'm not sure if that will do much good," said the Rat. "Toad will say anything for some peace."

Three quarters of an hour later, Mr Badger emerged, leading Toad. "I have here a sorry Toad," said Mr Badger. "He's going to give up motor-cars forever. I want you to repeat to your friends here how sorry you are and how silly it all was."

There was silence from Toad.

"I won't say I'm sorry," said Toad, at last. "I've thought about it now and I'm not sorry."

"Very well," said the Badger. "We'll have to try another way. Lock him in his room, while we sort something out."

The animals arranged to keep watch over the Toad until he had got over motor-cars. At first, Toad lined up chairs in the bedroom and using a dinner plate for a steering wheel, would imagine himself in charge of a magnificent motor-car. Gradually, this happened less often.

One fine morning, the Rat was on duty.

"Not much out of him this morning," the Badger said. "Very quiet and still in bed. That's when he is least likely to be trusted. So watch out!"

The Rat went into Toad. "How are you?" he asked. A feeble voice answered, "Oh, I'm all right."

"It's just the two of us until lunchtime," said the Rat.

"I'll try not to be any trouble," said Toad.

"You're no trouble," said the Rat. "We'll do what we can for you, Toady."

"If I thought that," sighed Toad, very weakly, "I'd ask you to pop to the village for me and fetch the doctor."

"Doctor, what for?" asked the Rat, beginning to feel a bit worried about Toad. He looked at him lying there, very still. "If you really want the doctor, I'll fetch him."

The Rat was very worried when he left Toad's room, but he didn't forget to lock the door.

Toad leapt out of bed as soon as he heard the key turn, he dressed himself quickly and with the help of several knotted sheets, he let himself out of his window and set off in the opposite direction to that taken by Rat.

The Rat realised his mistake as soon as he got back.

"Well, we can't do anything about it now," said the Badger. "We'll have to wait for him to be brought back – either on a stretcher or between two policemen."

Toad was meanwhile some miles away from home. He soon came to an inn, The Red Lion and remembering that he had not eaten breakfast that morning, Toad went in and ordered a large lunch. He was about half-way through, when he heard the all too familiar sound, coming down the street. Poop-poop! The sound came nearer and pulled up into the yard. The owners soon came into the inn.

Toad could stand the strain no longer. He paid his bill and went outside. There, in the yard, was a magnificent red motor-car.

Then as if in a dream, he was in the driver's seat, he had released the brake and was off! He swung the car out of the yard and down the road. He was the Terror of the High-way again!

The Judge looked down on the miserable Toad standing in the dock.

"To my mind," he said, "the only problem I see is how we punish the defendant for his crimes. Clerk, what is the stiffest penalty we can give the prisoner who has been found guilty of firstly, stealing a valuable motor-car, of secondly, dangerous driving and thirdly, some may say most seriously of all, cheeking the police?"

"For stealing the car, twelve months, I would suggest, my Lord. For dangerous driving, three years, but for the worst crime, cheeking the police, I would say a minimum of fifteen years. This would add up to ninteen years – so round it up to twenty years for good measure," said the clerk.

"Excellent," said the Judge. "Prisoner! Pull yourself together and try to stand up straight. It's twenty years for you this time, and if you ever appear before this court again, we shall deal most severely with you."

With that, Toad was dragged off to prison. He was locked in a cell, in an evil-smelling dungeon.

"This is the end," he sobbed, as he lay on his prison floor. "How can I hope to be set free? Imprisoned for stealing a motor-car and cheeking a red-faced policeman."

Toad carried on in such a way for several days, refusing to eat, even when the gaoler, knowing that Toad had some money, had pointed out that little luxuries could be sent in – at a price.

Now, the gaoler had a daughter who was fond of animals and couldn't bear to see Toad so upset.

"Please let me see him, Father," she said to the gaoler. "I'll bring him round."

The girl took him some food. "Come on, Toad,"

"Prisoner! Pull yourself together and try to stand up straight.
It's twenty years for you this time."

she said as she entered the cell.

The smell reached Toad, even as he lay in all his misery, but he would not be comforted, so the girl left, taking the food with her. The smell, however, lingered.

A few hours later, the girl came back with hot, buttered toast, the butter oozing through the bread. Toad sat up and ate the lot. He began to tell the girl about himself. Soon he began to feel more like the Toad of old.

The girl came every day and they had some very interesting chats, sitting in the cell and it gradually became clear to her that it was wrong to keep Toad in prison for what seemed to her to be a very minor offence.

"Toad," she said, on one visit. "Listen to me for a moment. I have an aunt who is a washerwoman."

"Never mind," said Toad.

"Do be quiet, Toad," said the girl. "This aunt comes and washes for the prisoners who can afford to have their laundry done. Now it occurs to me that you are rich and she is very poor. Now, if you were to ask her nicely, you could come to some agreement by which she will lend you her dress and bonnet and you can escape from gaol dressed as the washerwoman. You're very much like her – especially your figure.

"I hope not," said Toad, in a huff. "I have a very elegant figure for what I am."

"You are a proud and ungrateful animal," said the girl. "I was only trying to help you."

"Yes, yes, thank you," said Toad, hurriedly. "But are you suggesting that Toad of Toad Hall should go about the country dressed as a washerwoman?"

"That, or stay here as Toad," said the girl.

Toad realised he was in the wrong.

"I am indeed a stupid Toad," he said. "Ask your aunt if she would be kind enough to call. I am sure we will be able to arrange something to please us both."

The next evening, the girl arrived with her aunt. The dress, apron, shawl and bonnet were a good fit. The gold coins left on the table left little

34

to discuss. The only request she had was that she be left bound and gagged in the corner so that no one would think she helped.

The girl laughed as she dressed Toad in his new outfit. Tying up the bonnet under his chin, she said, "You look just like her. Now off you go and good luck."

Toad left the cell and walked through the corridors of the gaol with his knees shaking. But shortly it became clear that the washerwoman's outfit was the password through the various gates and barriers between the cells and the outside world.

At last, he had crossed the last courtyard and as he heard the sound of the last gate closing behind him, Toad knew that he was really free!

Dizzy with his success, he walked quickly towards the lights of the town, not knowing quite what he should do next, except get away from the area as soon as possible. As he walked along, he suddenly noticed some green and red lights a little way off and then he heard the chuff of steam engines.

"Aha!" he said. "What luck! I can take the train home."

He went into the station and joined the queue at the ticket office. As his turn came, he put his hand where his waistcoat pocket should be, only no pocket! Only the cotton dress that had served him so well! He had left his money in his waistcoat pocket back at the gaol cell.

He tried his bluff, toad voice. "Now look here, I've left my purse behind. Just give me the ticket and I will forward you the money. I'm well known in those parts."

"If you're that well-known," said the clerk. "It sounds to me like you've tried this trick before. So stand back and let me serve these other passengers."

Toad was very upset and with tears in his eyes he wandered down the platform where the train was standing. "So near and yet so far," he sobbed. "Only no money stops me from getting home." He knew his escape would soon be discovered. "Then

I'll be clapped in irons and dragged back to that dreadful place," he thought. He found himself standing near the driver of the train.

"Hullo, mother," he said. "What's the problem?"

"Oh, sir!" cried Toad, sobbing. "I am a poor unhappy widow washerwoman. I've lost my purse and I can't get home."

"Well, I'll tell you what," said the driver. "I go through my shirts at a fair rate and the wife would dearly love a rest from them. Suppose you take a bundle to wash and send on. I'll give you a ride on my engine."

Toad was delighted and leapt up on to the cab. Of course, he had never washed a shirt in his life and he had no intention of starting now. "I'll send him enough money to get any quantity washed," thought Toad, with a smile. "That's a better idea."

The guard blew the whistle and waved the flag and the train pulled slowly out of the station. As the train picked up speed, Toad could see on either side of him real fields, and trees, and hedges, and cows, and horses, all flying past, all the while thinking that every mile travelled brought him closer to home and to his friends. He would soon have a warm bed to sleep in, money in his pocket and good food to eat.

The miles were being eaten up and Toad was starting to think about supper when he noticed that the driver kept looking behind.

"It's strange," the driver said at last, "but I would swear that there is a train following us, and yet we're the last this evening."

Toad's heart sank; he knew exactly who was behind them.

The driver was still looking behind. "I can see it now," he said. "It's an engine following us and it seems to be full of policemen and detectives shouting 'Stop! Stop!'"

Toad was heartbroken, he fell to his knees in the coal dust.

"Please, dear kind engine driver, save me. I will tell you everything. I am not a washerwoman. I am

36

*Toad could see on either side of him real fields and trees,
and hedges, and cows, and horses, all flying past.*

the well-known Toad and I have escaped from the horrible cell that my enemies had thrown me in. They'll drag me back in chains and feed me on bread and water for the rest of my days. Please help me."

"Now, tell the truth, what did you do?" asked the driver, with a serious look on his face.

"Not very much," said Toad. "I borrowed a motor-car from people while they were at lunch; I didn't really mean to steal it, but that's how they looked at it."

"I don't like cars," said the driver. "And I don't like being ordered about by policemen when I'm on my own engine. So, don't worry, Toad, we'll do our best to get you away."

Toad helped to shovel the coal on and the engine picked up speed. But it was no good, the other engine was gaining on them.

"They have a better engine, Toad, and are pulling less weight," said the driver. "I've got an idea though. A little way ahead is a long tunnel. I'll put on all speed through the tunnel, the other train will slow down through fear of an accident, then at the other end I'll put the brakes on. You will have to jump out then and hide. I'll speed up then and they can chase me as much as they like."

They piled the coal on and the train sped through the tunnel. On the other side, the driver shut off the steam and slowed the train enough for Toad to jump clear and roll down the bank.

Toad then ran for the trees and hid. He watched as the train picked up speed again and then he saw the second train emerge from the tunnel, roaring and whistling, with its passengers all yelling, "Stop! Stop!"

Toad chuckled as he watched them go by, but he soon stopped when he realised that it was cold, dark and late and he didn't know where he was. He had no money and he was still far from home.

He spent a very cold, hungry, cramped night in the shelter of a hollow tree. He woke up as the morning sun shone on his east-facing shelter. For a moment he wondered where he was, where were the familiar walls and iron bars? Then he remembered his daring escape.

Free! The word alone made him feel warm. All he needed now was someone to tell him the way to go to get home. He set off and eventually came to a canal. As both the canal and the road ran in the same direction for a while, Toad followed the road, walking in the sunshine. Round the bend a horse plodded at an easy pace. Rope from the collar around his neck stretched across the water to a barge being pulled through the water. Toad let the horse pass and watched as the barge pulled up alongside him. Inside was a big, stout woman, wearing a linen bonnet, her strong, brown arm held the tiller.

"A nice morning, ma'am," she said to Toad, as she drew level.

"Nice for some, ma'am," replied Toad politely. "But not if you're in sore trouble like me. My married daughter sends for me to come as quick as you like, so I've had to leave my laundry business – I'm a washerwoman you see – and my youngest to look after themselves. Now I've lost my money and my way and as for what may be happening to my married daughter – as I say, it may be a nice morning for some."

"Where does your daughter live?" asked the bargewoman.

"Near the river, ma'am," said Toad, "close to a large house. I believe it's called Toad Hall."

"I know Toad Hall," exclaimed the bargewoman. "I'm on my way up past there. This canal joins the river nearby. You come with me and I can drop you off there."

She steered the barge to the bank and Toad stepped lightly on board and sat down.

"So you're in the laundry business, ma'am," said the bargewoman politely as they glided along. "A very good business, I should imagine. You must be very busy."

"I have girls working for me," said Toad. "But I have to keep an eye on them."

"Oh, I can imagine," said the bargewoman. "Do you

enjoy washing?"

"I love it," said Toad. "I couldn't live without it. Never happier than with my arms up to the elbows in soapsuds. A real pleasure, it is."

"Then what a stroke of luck it is meeting you," said the woman.

"It is?" said the Toad, nervously. "How do you mean?"

"Well, look at me," said the bargewoman. "Here I am in charge of this barge, while my husband goes in search of rabbit for the pot. 'Meet me at the next lock,' he says. And me, I like washing too, just like you, but how do I get the time to do it?"

"Never mind the washing," said Toad, trying to change the subject. "Think about the rabbit."

"All I can think of is my washing and how I can't do it," said the woman. "Tell you what, you go and grab some personal bits from the cabin and then you can do a spot of what you enjoy doing most. It would be a great help to me. All you need is down below, tub, soap and there's a kettle on the stove. I'll know you're enjoying yourself then."

Toad was cornered. He couldn't even jump to the bank to make a quick get away. "Well, so what," he thought, "Surely any fool can do the washing."

He fetched the soap, tub and water. He added a few odd items from the cabin and then tried to remember what he had seen through the odd laundry windows that he had bothered to look through.

Time passed and Toad became crosser and crosser. The clothes would just not do what he wanted. He looked over his shoulder once or twice, but the bargewoman seemed to be concentrating on the steering. Meanwhile, much to Toad's horror, his paws were going crinkly from being in so much water and to top it all he dropped the soap for what must have been the fiftieth time.

A sudden burst of laughter made him turn around. The bargewoman stood there, hands on hips, laughing with tears running down her face.

"Call yourself a washerwoman," she cried. "I'd say you've never even washed a dishcloth!"

40

Toad's temper, which he had been keeping under control, suddenly boiled over.

"You common bargewoman!" he shouted, "Don't you dare to talk to me like that. I would have you know that I am Toad, the well-known and distinguished Toad, not some washerwoman!"

The bargewoman peered closely at Toad. "Why so you are," she agreed. "You are indeed a horrible, nasty, crawly Toad. And in my nice clean barge. That I will not have!"

A moment later, she had hold of Toad by a front and back paw and he was suddenly sailing through the air, into the canal. He came up, spitting water, to see the bargewoman standing laughing at him.

"I'll get even," thought Toad, as he swam towards the bank.

Once on dry land, he hitched up his skirts and chased after the barge. He knew exactly what he was going to do. He ran swiftly and soon caught up with the barge horse. He untied the tow-rope jumped onto the horse's back and urged it into a gallop. He headed for open country, as he looked back, he could see the bargewoman waving her arms and yelling, "Stop! Stop!"

The barge horse was not built for speed and soon slowed down to a walk. Toad was quite happy. It was going the right way.

They ambled along in the warm sunshine and Toad was feeling quite drowsy, when the horse suddenly stopped and put its head down to graze. Toad woke with a start and just saved himself from falling. He looked around and saw that he was on an open green, close to a dingy, gipsy caravan. Outside, a man sat by a fire and a pot was hanging over it. The smell convinced Toad that what he felt earlier was not hunger. Now it was the real thing!

The gipsy was the first to speak. "Do you want to sell that horse of yours?" he asked.

Toad was completely taken aback. He did not know that gipsies were fond of horsedealing. But here was the opportunity to turn the horse into two things he needed – breakfast and money.

"Sell this beautiful horse of mine?" asked Toad. "But how would I get my laundry to my customers each week?"

"Try a donkey instead," suggested the gipsy.

"All the same, how much would you offer for him?" asked Toad.

The gipsy looked the horse over carefully. "A shilling a leg," he said at last.

"A shilling a leg," said Toad. "Give me a minute to work that out." After a while he said, "That's four shillings. I can't possibly sell my beautiful horse for such an amount."

"Well," said the gipsy. "Suppose I increase it to five shillings – that's three and six more than it's worth."

Toad sat and thought deeply. He was hungry, penniless and still some way from home. Five shillings would be very useful. At last he said, "Look here, how about you give me six shillings and sixpence, and as much breakfast from that pot as I can eat. Then the horse is yours. If not, I know someone close by who's been after this horse of mine for years."

The gipsy grumbled, but finally he lugged a dirty canvas bag out of the depths of his pocket. He then fetched a plate, spoon and fork and poured some of the rich hot stew out for Toad. It was indeed delicious and Toad ate until he was stuffed.

Toad eventually stood up and said goodbye to the gipsy, who very kindly gave directions for Toad to follow. Life had certainly changed for him in the last hour. He was now dry, heading for home. He had money in his pocket and a good hearty breakfast inside.

After some miles, the lane turned onto the high road and as he glanced along the road he spotted something distinctly familiar and then the too well-known 'Poop-poop!' fell on his ear.

"Oh, this is the real life," said the excited Toad. "I've been away from it for far too long. I will hail them, my brothers of the road, tell them my story and they will feel sorry enough for me to

He lugged a dirty canvas bag out of the depths of his pocket.

give me a lift. And who knows, a spot more talk and I may be able to drive right up to Toad Hall! That will be one in the eye for Badger!"

Toad stood and watched the approaching car, as it slowed down. But then his heart sank, his knees turned to water and he gradually turned very pale. The car that was coming towards him was the same car that he had stolen at the Red Lion, that fatal day when his troubles began.

Toad sank to the ground. "It's all over," he thought, "I'll be dragged back in chains, back to that cell. Oh Toad, why couldn't you go home by the back lanes instead of dancing along the main road?"

The car pulled up and stopped.

"It looks like a washerwoman," said one of the occupants. "Poor thing, maybe the heat is too much for her and she's fainted. Let's take her to the nearest village."

Toad was gently lifted into the car and propped against some cushions. When he heard what they said, he knew he had not been recognised. He cautiously opened one eye and then the other.

"There look," said one gentleman. "She looks better already."

"I may feel better, kind sir," said Toad in a weak voice. "If I may be allowed to sit in the front seat with the fresh air full on my face."

"Of course, you're absolutely right," he said.

A few minutes later, a very happy Toad was sitting in the front seat, next to the driver.

"Why fight it?" he thought to himself. Aloud, he spoke to the driver. "Please sir," he said. "Would you very kindly allow me to drive your car?" The driver laughed and the gentlemen asked what the matter was. When they heard Toad's request, they replied, to Toad's delight, "Bravo, ma'am! Let her have a go. She can't do any harm!"

Toad scrambled into the driver's seat and appeared to listen carefully to the instructions. Then he set off very carefully and very slowly.

"How well she drives!" cried the gentlemen. "Fancy a washerwoman being able to drive so well, first time too!"

Toad went a little faster and then faster still

"Careful, washerwoman," said the driver. This annoyed Toad.

He put his foot down and the car went even faster. The driver tried to interfere but Toad held him off with one arm. The rush of the air and the noise of the engine were making him very excited.

"Washerwoman indeed!" he yelled. "Ho, ho! I am Toad, the motor-car thief, the gaol-breaker, Toad who always escapes!"

The car's occupants immediately threw themselves at Toad. "Stop him! Tie him up!" they cried. With a quick turn of the wheel, Toad sent the car crashing through a hedge, into a pond.

Toad went flying through the air and landed on thick grass. He picked up his skirts and ran, scrambling through hedges and across fields. He slowed down after a while when he saw that nobody was following him.

"Ho! Ho!" he giggled. "Toad has come out on top again! How clever I . . ."

A sudden noise made him look behind. About two fields away he could see two burly policemen and the driver running towards him.

"Oh, foolish Toad!" he cried. "Boasting again."

Toad picked up his skirts and began to run, but he was not as fast as those who were following him and they were getting closer. He looked back to see how close they were when the ground disappeared beneath his feet.

Splash! He was in the river!

He tried to grab at the reeds on the bank, but the river carried him past. He went down again and came up by a large hole. He grabbed at the edge and held on. Bit by bit he pulled himself up on the bank and lay there spluttering.

Something moved in the hole and there were two twinkling eyes looking at him. He gradually made out a face – a familiar face! Brown and small with whiskers. Such a glossy coat, such neat ears!

It was the Water Rat!

'Like Summer Tempests Came His Tears'

The Rat put out his paw and grabbed Toad by the scruff of the neck. Soon a water-logged Toad stood in the Rat's Hall, dripping weed and water. But he was in the home of a friend. He was free!

"Oh Ratty," he cried. "What a time I've had. Been in gaol . . ."

"Toad, be quiet," said the Rat. "Go upstairs and get out of that rag that looks as though it belongs to a washerwoman. Have a good wash and find something of mine to wear. Now off you go!"

Toad wanted to talk but then he saw himself in a mirror and thought better of it. He had a good wash and dressed in the Rat's slightly smaller clothes and stood before the mirror, wondering how anyone could have mistaken him for a washerwoman.

Toad went downstairs to a full-blown lecture from the Rat. Toad had to admit that the Rat was right.

"But as I was hanging on to your hole, a thought came to me about motor-boats. Let's not discuss it eh, Ratty," said Toad hurriedly as the Rat began to stamp his foot. "Let's have a coffee and stroll down to Toad Hall."

"Stroll down to Toad Hall!" cried the Rat excitedly. "Haven't you heard?"

"Heard? Heard what?" asked Toad, turning pale.

"You mean you've heard nothing about the Stoats and Weasels!" cried the Rat.

"The Wild Wooders?" cried Toad. "No, what have they done?"

"They've taken over Toad Hall, that's what!" shouted the Rat.

"How did it happen?" asked Toad, in a small voice. "Tell me the worst."

"Well, when you got into your spot of trouble," began the Rat. "We River-bankers all stood up for you. But the Wild Wooders said it served you right. Well, Mole and Badger moved into the Hall to look out for it until you came home, as we all knew you should. One night, a whole gang of ferrets, stoats and weasels attacked the Hall and threw Moly and Badger out. What could they do? They were two, unarmed, against hundreds. They've been there ever since, making a right mess and they're telling everyone that they're there to stay."

"They are, are they?" said Toad getting up and grabbing a stick. "I'll soon see about that!"

"It's no good, Toad," the Rat called after him.

But Toad was off. He marched down the road and up to the front gate of the Hall, when a ferret popped out from behind a pillar.

The ferret said nothing. He just raised the gun he was holding and pointed it towards Toad. Toad fell flat on the ground. Bang! The bullet whistled over his head. He returned to the Rat very crestfallen.

"I did try to tell you," said the Rat. "The whole place is surrounded. We'll just have to wait."

Toad was still not about to give up. He got out the boat and headed down the river. He came up to Toad Hall and all seemed quiet and peaceful. Very warily he paddled up to the mouth of the creek, and was just passing under the bridge, when . . . CRASH! A great stone, dropped from the bridge, and smashed

Very warily he paddled up to the mouth of the creek
and was just passing under the bridge, when . . . Crash!

through the bottom of the boat. He looked up to
see two stoats, laughing away. "Your head, next
time, Toady!" one called.

Toad swam to the bank and returned to the Rat.

"What did I say?" said the Rat crossly. "You've
lost my boat and spoilt a good suit of clothes – I
wonder you've any friends left."

Toad was very apologetic. "I will do nothing
without your say so from now on," he said.

"Let's have some supper, as it's getting late."
said the Rat. "Then we'll hear what Mole and Badger
have to say."

"Of course, Mole and Badger," said Toad, "How are
they?"

"You may well ask," said the Rat sharply. "Those
two have been camping out, planning how to get
your house back for you. You don't deserve such
friends really."

"You're right," said the Toad. "I should go out
and find them right now. Is that supper, Ratty?"

The Rat remembered Toad had been on prison
rations for a while and was probably hungry. He
followed him to the table and served him what he
wanted. They had just finished eating when there
was a very heavy knock at the door.

It was Badger. His shoes were muddy and his
clothes were scruffy. He walked up to Toad and
shook his paw. "Welcome home, Toad," he said.
"What am I saying? This is a poor homecoming."

Then he sat and helped himself to a large slice
of pie.

Toad was alarmed at the greeting.

"Never mind Badger," said the Rat. "He'll be all
right when he's eaten."

Some time later, a lighter knock came at the
door. It was the Mole.

"Hooray! Here's old Toad!" he cried. "We never
thought you'd be home so soon. Why, you must have
escaped, you clever Toad."

Toad started to visibly puff and swell.

"Clever? Me?" he said. "No, not really, not
according to some of my friends, anyway. Still,
I only broke out of prison, escaped the police,

captured a train. I disguised myself as I went about the country, fooling everyone. I'm a stupid fool. I'll tell you some of my adventures, Mole and you can judge for yourself."

"Well, tell me while I'm eating, I've had nothing to eat since breakfast."

Toad stood, legs apart, on the hearth rug, thrust his paw into his trouser-pocket and pulled out a handful of silver.

"Do you know how I got this?" he asked the Mole. "Horse-stealing. Just a few second's work."

"Quiet, Toad," said the Rat. "Look Mole, what's happening out there and what should we do, now Toad is back?"

"Well, it's about as bad as it can be," said the Mole. "And as to what we should do, I don't really know. Mr Badger and I have been round and round the Hall and there are sentries everywhere and they stand and laugh at us."

"Well, it seems to me," began the Rat. "Now that Toady's back, he should . . ."

"Oh, no," cried the Mole, with his mouth full. "He should do something totally different."

"Well, I'm not going to do either," said Toad. "I'm not going to be told by you two what to do."

All three were by now talking and shouting at once but another voice was heard through it. "Be quiet at once, all of you!" Everyone was instantly silent. Without another word he reached for the cheese. Such was the respect for the Badger, that not another word was said until the Badger had completed his meal.

When the Badger had finished, he stood before the fireplace. At last he spoke.

"Toad!" he said sharply. "You really are a most ungrateful creature. Aren't you ashamed of yourself?"

Toad let out a sob.

"Now, now, there's no need to cry!" said the kindly Badger. "But Mole is right, you know. We're not going to get Toad Hall back by storming the place. There are far too many of them."

"Then it's all over," sobbed Toad. "I may never

50

Toad stood, legs apart, on the hearth rug,
thrust his paw into his trouser-pocket and pulled out a handful of
silver.

see Toad Hall again."

"Cheer up, Toad," said the Badger. "There are other ways to get Toad Hall back than by storming it. Now, I'm going to tell you something that has been a great secret for a long time."

Toad loved secrets and his tears soon dried.

"There is an underground passage," said the Badger. "It leads from the riverbank, right up into Toad Hall."

"Nonsense, Badger," said Toad. "I know every inch of that place and there are absolutely no secret passages."

"My dear young friend," said the Badger quietly. "Your father was a good friend of mine and he told me many things that he knew he couldn't entrust to you. This was one of them. He found the passage one day, cleaned it out and repaired it. He showed it to me, saying, 'Don't let my son know about it. He's a good boy, but inclined to chatter. It wouldn't stay a secret for long. If he's ever in a real fix and it is of use to him, tell him about the secret passage, but not before.'"

"How is this secret passage going to help us?" asked Toad.

"I've found out a thing or two in the last couple of days," said the Badger. "I had the Otter dress himself up as a chimney sweep. He got as far as the back door, asking for work. He heard that there's going to be a big party tomorrow night. Someone's birthday, Chief Weasel, I think – all the weasels will be in the dining room, eating and drinking and not a single weapon between them. They'll think they're safe there."

"But there will be guards as usual, won't there?" asked the Rat.

"Of course," said the Badger. "And the partygoers will have absolute faith in them. As for the passage. That comes up right next to the dining room."

"That squeaky board!" said Toad.

"We creep in," said the Mole.

"With our pistols and swords and sticks," shouted the Rat.

"And we rush in upon them," said the Badger.
"And whack 'em and whack 'em and whack 'em!"
cried Toad.

"Right then," said the Badger, in a quieter
voice. "It's all settled. There's nothing more to
argue about. We can all go to bed and make the
final arrangements in the morning."

Toad went quietly to his bed, the first time
between the sheets for a long time, thinking that
he was too excited to sleep. But it had been an
eventful day and he was soon fast asleep,
dreaming. It was all a bit of a muddle, as dreams
tend to be, but he did remember seeing a barge
sailing into his dining room with the week's
washing on board, just as he was giving a dinner
party for all his friends.

He slept late and when he eventually went
downstairs, the Badger was sitting reading the
newspaper as if it were an ordinary morning and not
one when they were planning to take the weasels by
surprise. The Mole was nowhere to be seen. He had
disappeared very early saying he had an errand.

The Rat meanwhile was counting out the arms and
weapons for that night. He ran here and there
making four piles of weapons.

"A sword for Rat, a sword for Mole, a sword for
Badger and a sword for Toad," he said excitedly.
"A pistol for Rat, a pistol for Mole, a pistol for
Badger and a pistol for Toad!"

The four piles grew.

"Really, Ratty," began the Badger, as he looked
up from his newspaper. "I don't think you're going
to need that lot. One stout stick each and that
will be enough to teach those ferrets and weasels
a lesson."

"Better safe than sorry," said the Rat.

Toad had finished his breakfast as the Mole
walked in the door.

"I've just had such fun with the stoats," he said
as he fell into a chair, laughing.

"I hope you've been careful," said the Rat.

"I should hope so, too," said the Mole. "I got
the idea when I saw that blue dress of Toad's

hanging in front of the fire this morning. I put it on and went off to Toad Hall. The sentries were all there and made their usual 'Who's there?' comments. 'Good morning, gentlemen,' says I. 'Want any washing done today?' 'We don't do washing on duty!' says they. 'Or any other time,' says I."

Toad was feeling exceedingly jealous of the Mole. It was just the sort of thing that he should have done.

"'Don't hold my men up with your chatter,' says the sergeant," continued the Mole. "'Now run along.' 'It won't be me running along later on today!' says I."

The Badger put his paper down.

"I could see they were listening to me," said the Mole. "The sergeant said, 'Never mind her. She doesn't know what she's talking about.' 'Well,' says I. 'My daughter works for that Mr Badger and she heard that a hundred bloodthirsty badgers are going to attack Toad Hall tonight and there'll be six boat loads of rats with pistols coming up the river and handpicked toads known as die-hards will attack through the orchard.' Then I ran away and hid in a ditch to see what would happen. I could see them getting nervous, complaining about the weasels having all the fun while they were going to be attacked by bloodthirsty badgers!"

"Mole," said the Badger. "I can see you have more sense in your little finger than most animals have in the whole of their fat little bodies. Well done, Mole!"

Toad was beside himself with jealousy, more so because he couldn't work out why the Mole had been so clever, and to get such praise from the Badger. Before he could say anything, the bell rang for lunch.

After lunch, the Badger settled down for a rest. The Rat carried on sorting out the weapons.

That left Mole and Toad. The Mole kindly led Toad outside and asked him to relate all his adventures from start to finish. Toad was delighted to do so, even if some of the stories did grow with the telling.

The Return of the Hero

When it was dark the Rat called them all together and stood them each next to a pile of weapons. Each animal was given a belt, with a sword on one side and a cutlass on the other. There was a pile of pistols, a truncheon, handcuffs, bandages, a flask and a sandwich case for each one.

"Really, Ratty," said the Badger, "I'll be much happier with just my stick. But I'll carry this lot to please you."

When they were all ready, Badger led the way along the bank.

"Right, Mole first, because I'm pleased with him. Then Rat and Toad brings up the rear," said Badger.

Toad did not want to be left out, so he made no fuss about his lowly position in the expedition. He followed closely behind the Rat. The Badger suddenly swung himself into a hole in the bank. The Mole and the Rat silently followed. But when it came to Toad's turn, he managed to slip into the water with a loud splash. The Badger was very angry.

"Next time, you'll be left behind," said the Badger.

But they were in the secret passage at last!

It was cold, damp, dark and low, Toad did not like it. He ran to keep up with Rat and bumped into him, the Rat collided with the Mole, who bumped into Badger.

That's it!" he said angrily. "This time that tiresome animal will be left behind!"

Toad whimpered a great deal and the Mole and the Rat promised that they would take care of the Toad and keep him out of the Badger's way. At last the Badger was pacified and the line was re-organised, this time with the Rat bringing up the rear, with a heavy paw on Toad's shoulder.

They clambered along the passageway.

"We should be underneath Toad Hall by now," said the Badger.

As if to prove that they were, all of a sudden they could hear distinct murmurings and stampings above their heads.

The passage began to slope upwards and the noise became clearer. "Come on," said the Badger and he led the way to a trapdoor.

There was so much noise going on that there was no chance of them being overheard. "Right boys, all together!" said the Badger and the four put their shoulders to the trap door and pushed. The pantry door was the only thing between them and the partying weasels. The cheering and hammering died down and a voice was heard saying, "Well, I won't keep you much longer but I think we should say a kind word to our absent host, Toad!"

"Just let me at him," said Toad, through clenched teeth.

"Hold on a second," said the Badger. "Are we all ready?"

"Let me sing you a song about our absent host," continued the voice from the next room.

"The hour is come," cried the Badger. "Follow me!"

What a squealing and a squeaking and a screeching filled the air!

The terrified weasels dived under the tables. They made mad leaps for the windows and curtains as the four heroes strode into the room. The mighty Badger, his great stick sweeping through the air! The Mole, black and grim, brandishing both sword and stick. The Rat, his belt bristling with all manner of weapons and Toad mad with anger, swollen to twice his normal size, ran straight for the terrified Chief Weasel. There may have only been four of them, but to the panic-stricken weasels it seemed that the Hall was full of monstrous animals yelling and whooping. The weasels fled with cries of terror, this way and that, through windows and up the chimney, to get out of the reach of those dreadful sticks!

The battle was soon over. The four friends strode up and down the Hall, whacking their sticks at everything that moved.

"Mole, go and see what those sentries are doing. I've an idea that, thanks to you, they won't be causing too much trouble."

The Mole disappeared through a window and the others set about straightening a table and sorting out supper.

"Stir your stumps, Toad," said the Badger. "We've got your house back for you."

They bustled around, Toad feeling a bit put out that again the Mole had been praised. He had attacked the Chief Weasel and sent him flying and no-one was congratulating him. They found some untouched food and were just about to sit down when the Mole came back with an armful of weapons.

"It's all over out there," he told them. "As far as I can tell, as soon as the stoats heard the noise from here, some of them just threw down their rifles and fled. Some stood their ground, but when the weasels came rushing out, they thought they were betrayed and began fighting each other. The weasels fought to get away and most of them ended up rolling in the river! They've all gone now, one way or another and I've got their rifles!"

"Excellent, Mole!" said the Badger. "Now, I have one more task before you sit down. Take these prisoners upstairs and have them clean out some bedrooms. Then send them away, we shouldn't have any more trouble with them. Then join us for some of this excellent tongue. I'm very pleased with you, Mole!"

The Mole led his troop of workers up the stairs. He returned a short time later, smiling, saying that every room was ready. "I didn't have to do anything," he added. "They all apologised and blamed the Chief Weasel and the stoats. So I gave them a bread roll each and sent them off."

Toad put all jealousy from him. "Thank you, dear Mole, for all your trouble tonight and for being so clever this morning."

The four friends strode up and down the hall,
whacking their sticks at everything that moved.

"Well said, Toad," said the Badger.

That night was spent once more between clean sheets, at Toad Hall.

The Toad was late down for breakfast as usual and came down to cold toast and luke-warm coffee and not much else; he wasn't too happy as it was his house after all. He could see the Mole and the Rat sitting out by the lawn, obviously telling each other stories and roaring with laughter. The Badger was reading the newspaper.

"You're going to be busy this morning," the Badger told the Toad. "You see, we really ought to give a banquet to celebrate."

"Of course," said Toad. "Anything to oblige. Though why this morning, I can't understand."

"Not this morning," replied the Badger, crossly. "What I mean is, invitations will have to be written and you've got to do them. Now there's a pile of headed paper on that desk, so sit down now and get writing. Don't worry, I'll help. I'll order the banquet."

"What, this very morning?" cried Toad. "But I want to get out and walk round the estate and sort things out. But, no – hang on, you're right, Badger, absolutely right. You order the banquet, anything you want and I'll take care of the invitations right now."

The Badger looked at him suspiciously, he left the room and as soon as the door was closed, Toad hurried to the table and began to think about the invitations. He could make some speeches and maybe sing one of his songs. Oh, this certainly would be an enjoyable evening!

He was delighted with the idea and got to work, finishing all the invitations by noon. He was informed that a small and slightly bedraggled weasel was at the front door who would be delighted to help any of the fine gentlemen if he could. Toad handed over the invitations and sent him off to deliver them.

Lunch was a short time later. The Mole was expecting to find a miserable Toad, having been left on his own all morning. Instead Toad was very bouncy and in good spirits.

The Mole was suspicious and the Rat and the Badger exchanged knowing glances. As soon as lunch was over, Toad headed for the garden, saying, "Ask for anything you want." He wanted to go and practise his speeches and songs. The Rat took his arm and led him towards the study.

"Now, look here, Toad," said the Rat. "It's about this banquet. We want you to understand once and for all, that there will be no speeches and songs. There'll be no arguments."

Toad's dream was shattered. "Just one little song?" he pleaded.

"No, not one," said the Rat, firmly.

Toad left the room, handkerchief to his face.

"Oh, Badger," said the Rat. "I feel so mean."

"I know, I know," said the Badger. "But it had to be done. Would you have him to be a laughing stock, jeered at by stoats and weasels?"

"And speaking of weasels," said the Rat. "It's a good job we met that little weasel with Toad's invitations. They were disgraceful. Mole is writing some more out now."

The hour for the banquet drew near and Toad was sitting in his bedroom. He sat thinking for a while, then stood before the mirror. There he stood and in his own Toad way, he gave all the speeches and sang all the songs that he had intended for the banquet. His audience of one, himself, loved every single word!

He then went downstairs for the banquet. All the animals cheered as he walked into the room. They congratulated him, but Toad said gentle things like, "Badger was the mastermind. Mole and Rat did most of the fighting. I just served in the ranks."

The meal was the best that could be served and throughout Toad made small talk with his neighbours. He was delighted that every time he looked at the Badger or the Rat, their mouths hung open in disbelief at his immaculate behaviour! Even when speeches were called for, Toad gently declined.

He was indeed an altered Toad!